P9-BIQ-675

Copyright © 2011 Flowerpot Press, a Division of Kamalu, LLC, Franklin, TN, U.S.A.
and Mitso Media, Inc., Oakville, ON, Canada
PRINTED IN CHINA

All rights reserved. No part of this publication may be reproduced, stored in a retrieval system or
transmitted by any means, electronic, mechanical, photocopying or
otherwise, without the prior permission of the publisher.

Daisy, Daisy

Illustrated by Nicole Groot

Special thanks to, Anthony Findley,
for helping a young artist find a publisher.

This is the tale of a dog,
not the *tail* of a dog you understand,
but the tale of a dog.

This dog's name is Davey McGrew.

All of his life Davey McGrew
    spent all of his time with nothing to do.

He would lay about town,
    maybe stare into the blue,

or whistle on the wind
    as the clouds rolled through.

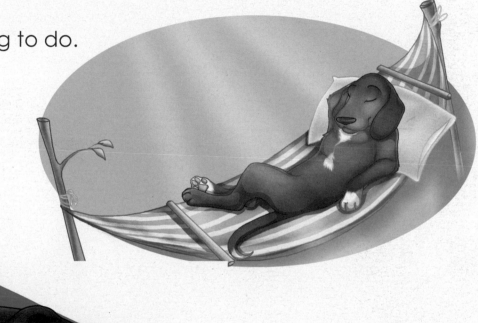

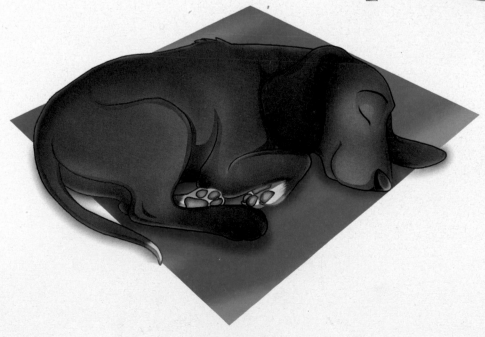

One day the life of Davey McGrew turned upside-down and spun around.
A girl walked by that made Davey's heart pound.

She was the most beautiful girl that he'd ever found.

This girl's name was Daisy Bell.

Daisy was something incredibly swell.
She was pretty and nice, and she had a fine smell.
Why, just look at her here; it is easy to tell.

Davey jumped up and went off in pursuit.
He must meet this dog; she's so incredibly cute.
Daisy Bell just kept walking,
ignoring his talking,
until her ears started ringing
when young McGrew started singing.

And he would sing to her...

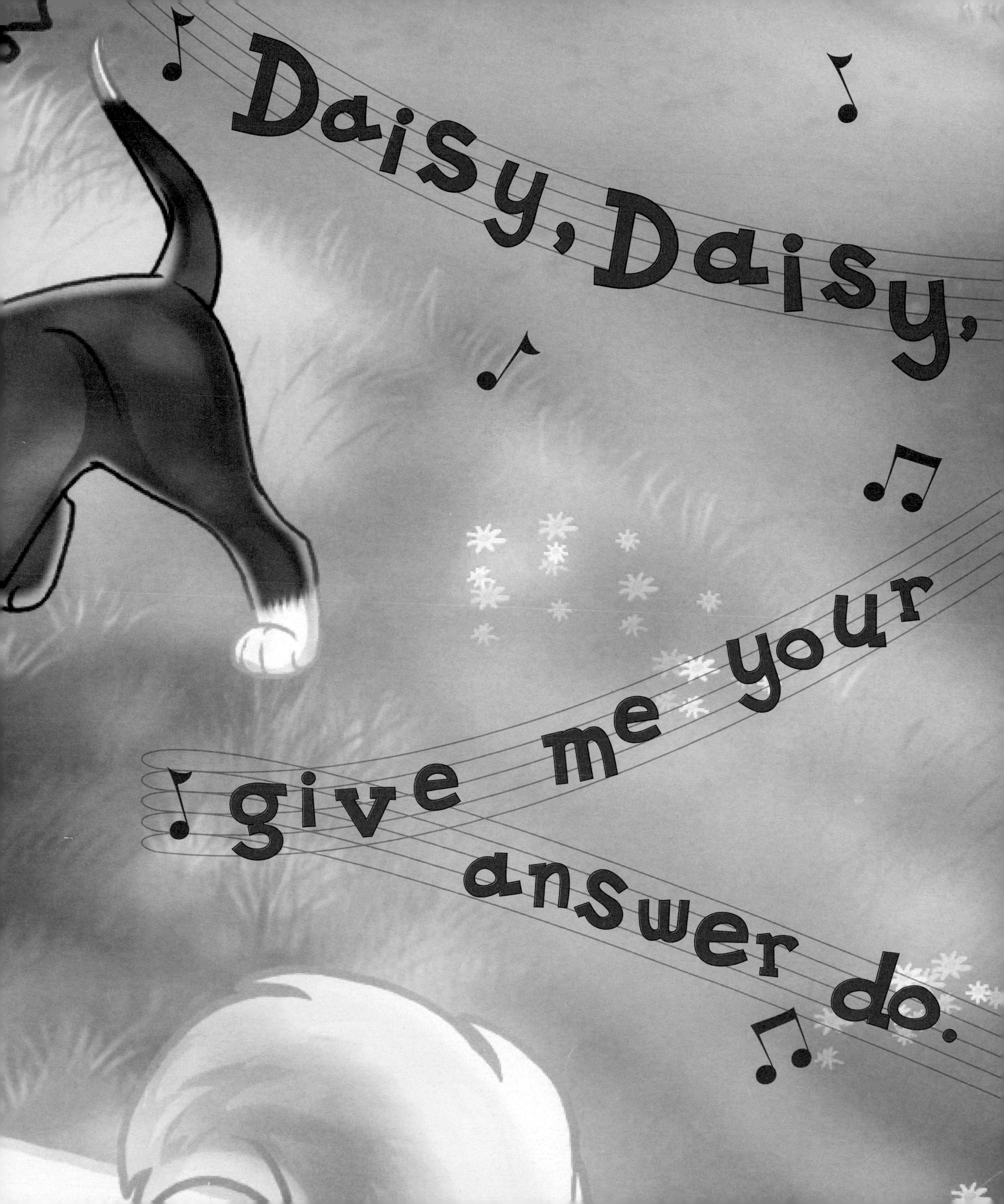

Daisy, Daisy, give me your answer do.

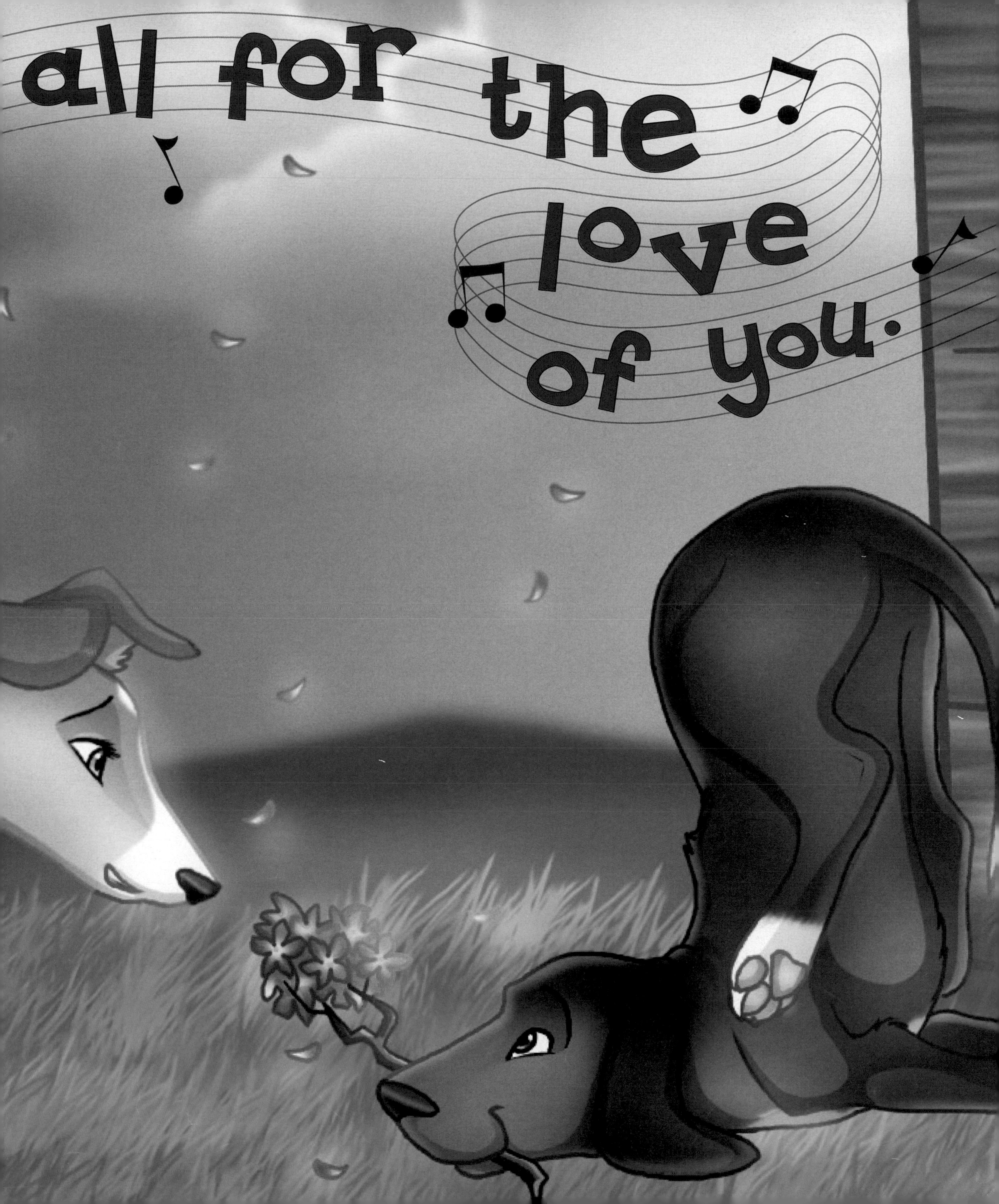

all for the love of you.

stylish marriage.

afford a carriage.

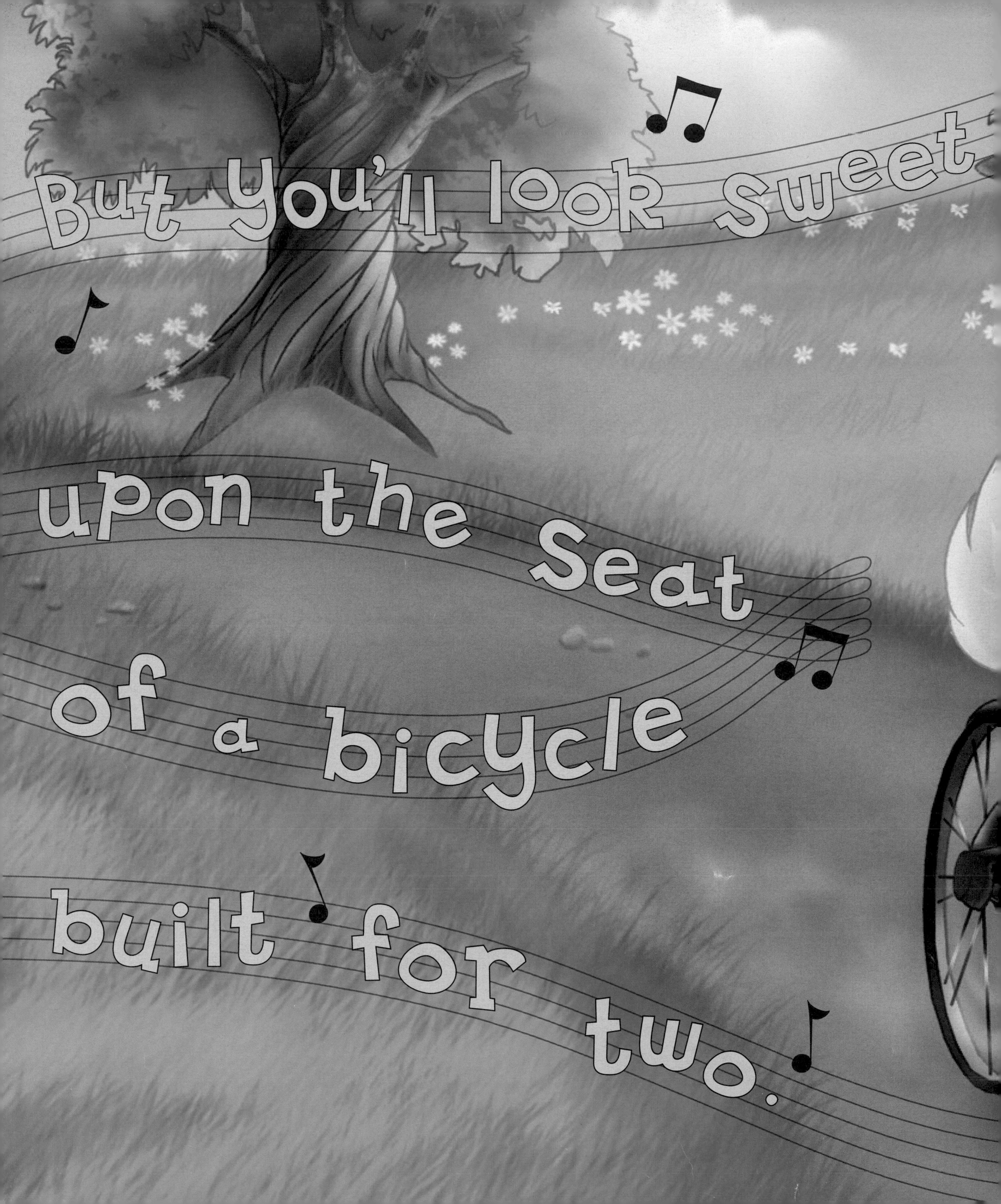

But you'll look sweet
upon the seat
of a bicycle
built for two.

There is a flower within my heart, Daisy Daisy. Planted one

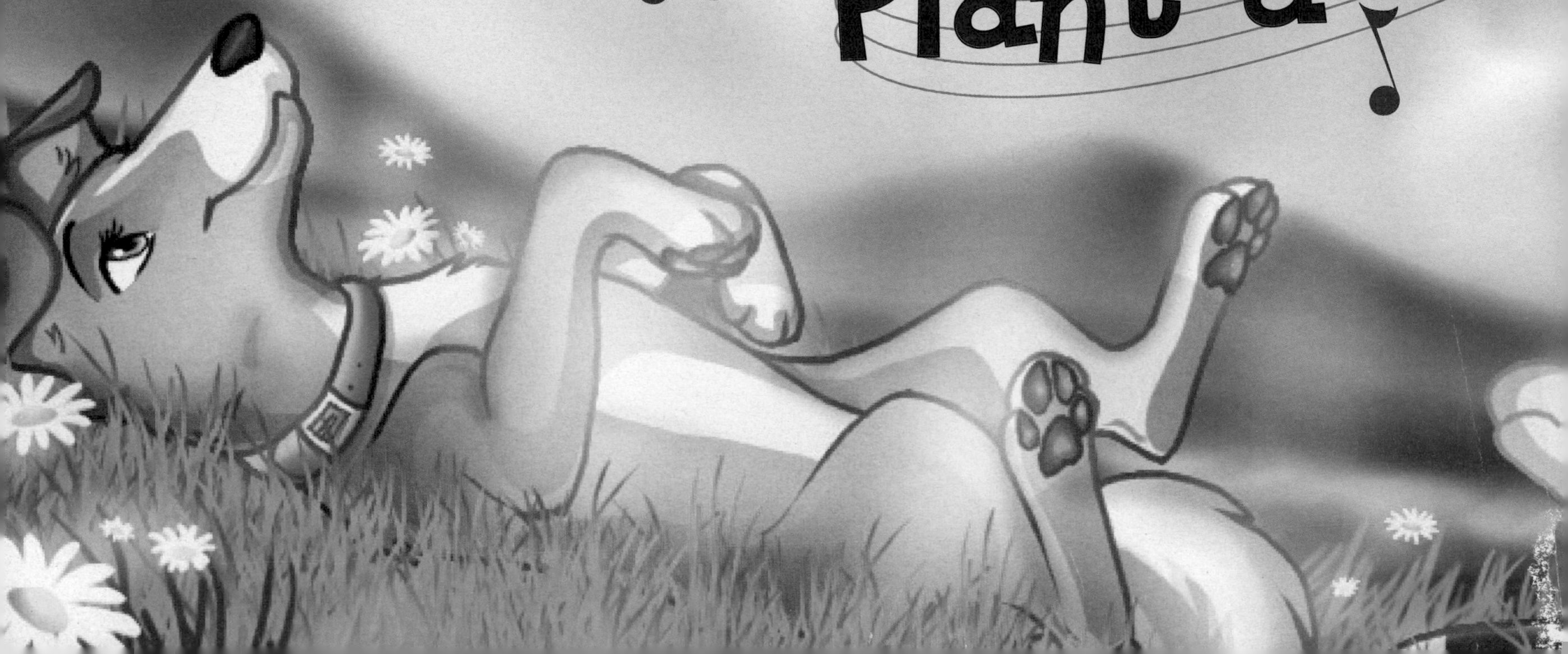

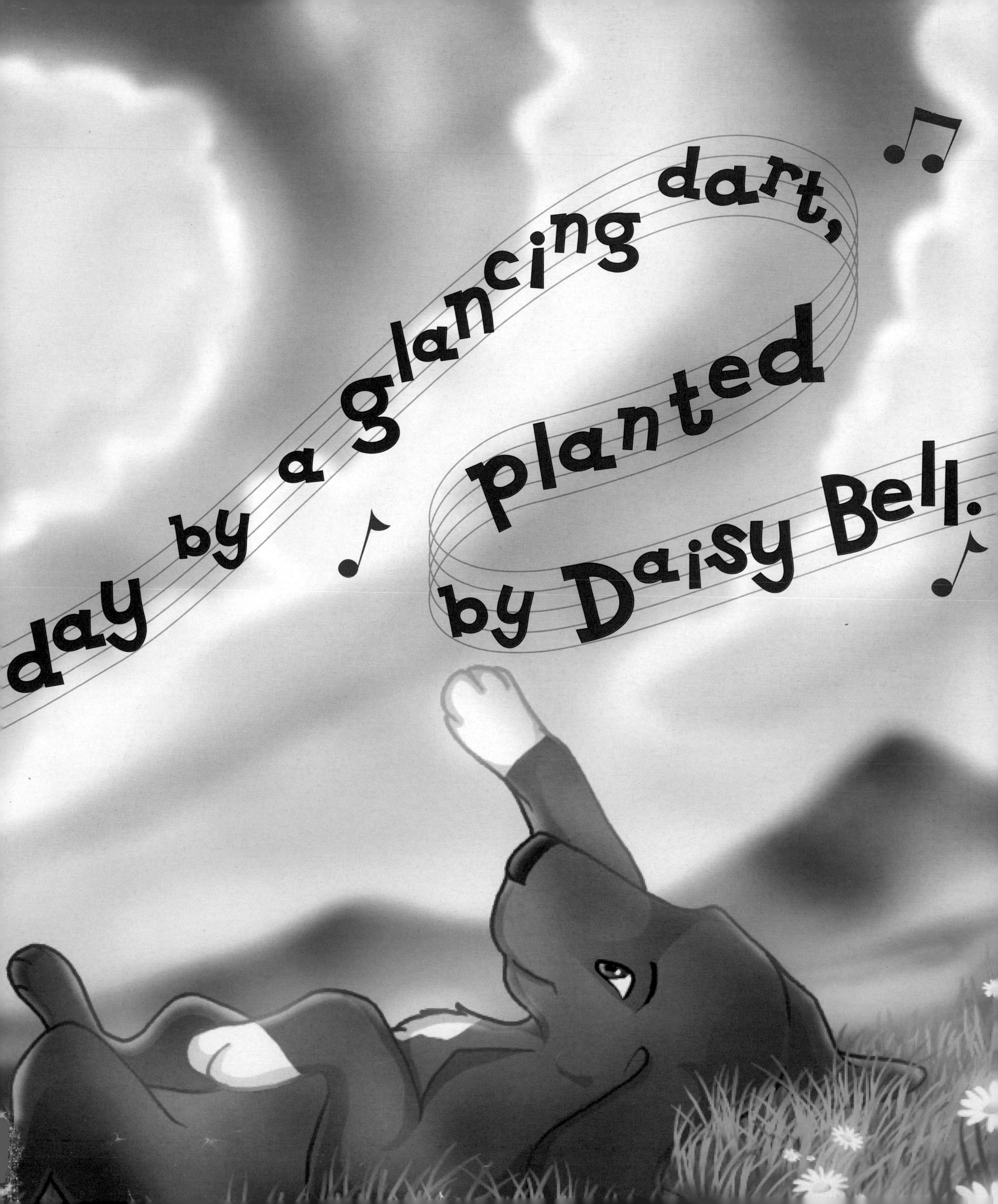

day by a glancing dart,
planted by Daisy Bell.

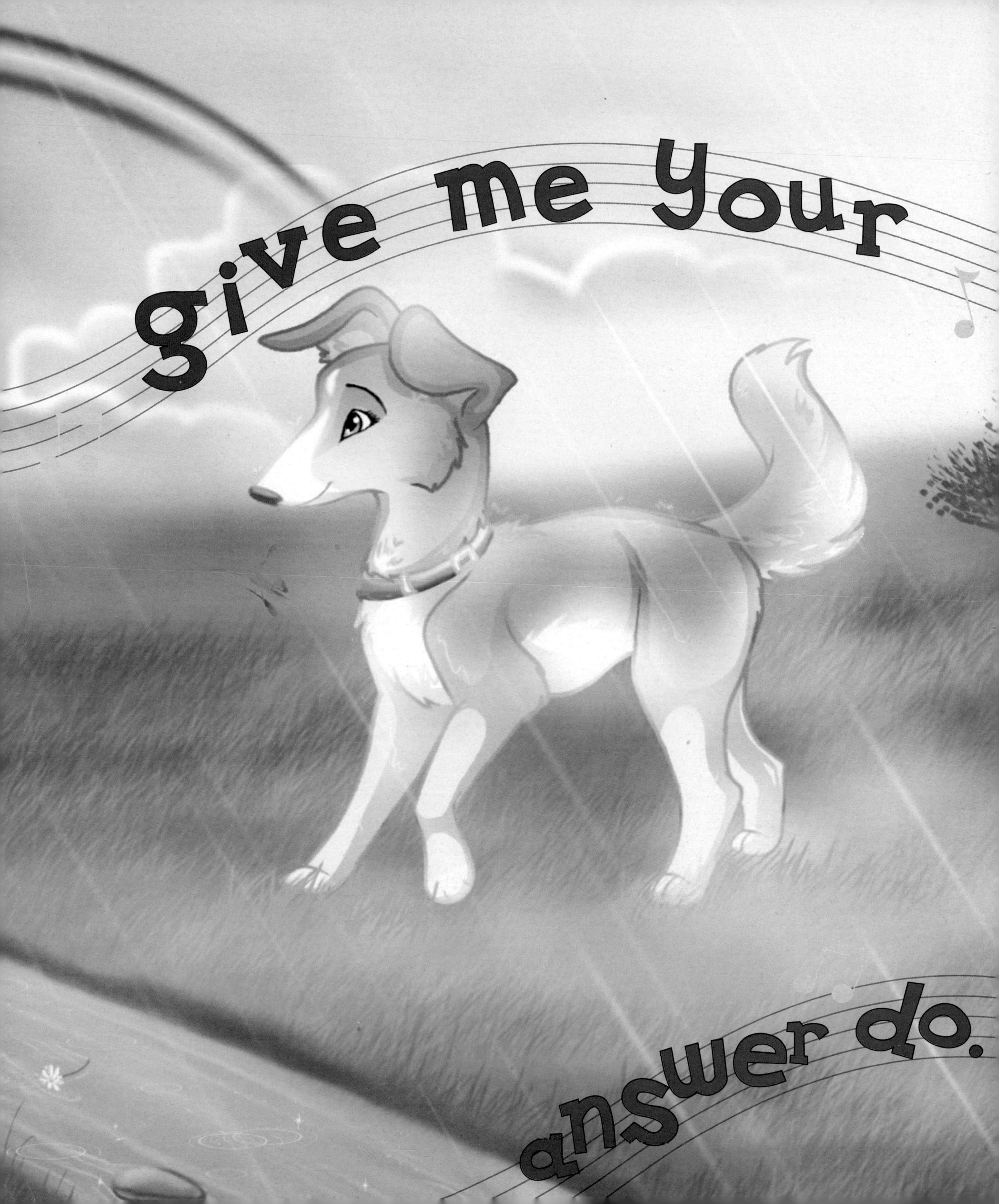

give me your

answer do.

a carriage.

After lots of running and lots of singing,
Daisy slowed down and gave Davey a look.
Davey slowed, too, and gave Daisy a flower,
and then a big smile. And that's all it took.

From that day forward they spent their days together
talking and laughing and doing what they like.
If you look you will find them. They are not hard to notice.
Just keep an eye out for two dogs on a bike.

That is not where this dog's tale ends,
because Daisy and Davey became more than just friends.
They married and later had two girls and a son.
Their marriage, though not too stylish, was very pretty and quite fun.

Now they live out their lives filled with love and laughter...
and these two friendly dogs will live happily ever after.

THE END